ARY FILES

Secrets and Lies

Paul Blum

RISING STARS

'The truth is inside us.
It is the only place where it can hide.'

nasen

NASEN House, 4/5 Amber Business Village, Amber Close,
Amington, Tamworth, Staffordshire B77 4RP

Rising Stars UK Ltd.
22 Grafton Street, London W1S 4EX
www.risingstars-uk.com

Text © Rising Stars UK Ltd.
The right of Paul Blum to be identified as the author of this work has
been asserted by him in accordance with the Copyright, Design and
Patents Act 1988.

Published 2007

Cover design: Button plc
Illustrator: Aleksandar Sotiroski
Text design and typesetting: pentacor**big**
Publisher: Gill Budgell
Editor: Maoliosa Kelly
Editorial consultant: Lorraine Petersen and Cliff Moon

British Library Cataloguing in Publication Data.
A CIP record for this book is available from the British Library.

ISBN: 978-1-84680-249-2

Printed by Craft Print International Limited, Singapore

CHAPTER ONE

The Lake District, Northern England

It was a foggy night. A car was speeding along the roads in the Lake District. Suddenly a bright light shone down from the sky and the driver was blinded. The car skidded out of control and crashed.

Robert Parker and Laura Turnbull were British Secret
Service Agents. They worked for MI5 and were
working at the scene of the crash.

"This is not just a car crash," said Agent Parker. "The car has melted and I can't see any dead bodies. We need to ask some questions," he said. "We need to speak to the Head of the Crash Team."

The Head of the Crash Team was puzzled as well.

"I don't understand what's happened here. There are no bodies and the car looks like it has melted."

"No bodies and a melted car? I think this may be a case of alien abduction," said Agent Parker.

"I don't think so," said the Head of the Crash Team. "This is the real world. I've worked in this business for 20 years and I haven't seen any little green monsters from outer space yet."

"Okay, thanks for your help," Turnbull said. "We'll get back to you if we need anything else."

The next morning, Parker got a call on his mobile phone.

"The local police have picked up a woman who says she was driving the melted car," said Parker.

"We need to speak to her. Let's go!" said Turnbull.

CHAPTER TWO

At the police station they met Mrs Chivers, the driver. She had a blanket wrapped around her and she was drinking a cup of tea.

The agents showed the police officer their identity cards.

"I'm Agent Turnbull. This is my partner, Agent Parker. We work for MI5. We'd like to speak to this woman alone in an interview room," said Turnbull.

"Good luck to you," replied the police officer. He winked at Turnbull and Parker and whispered, "You'll need it with this one. She's completely mad."

They went into the interview room and Mrs Chivers told them her story.

"There was a bright light. I saw a spaceship in the sky. Then I felt myself being lifted from the car. The next thing I knew, I was lying down on a table."

"I had wires attached to my head and there were strange green monsters looking at me. They seemed very excited. Suddenly, there was a big bang and everything went dark. When I woke up, I found myself walking on the road."

Just then, Turnbull's mobile phone rang. She took the call.

"That was the Head of the Crash Team. He wants to see us again. He sounds very worried," she said.

12

CHAPTER THREE

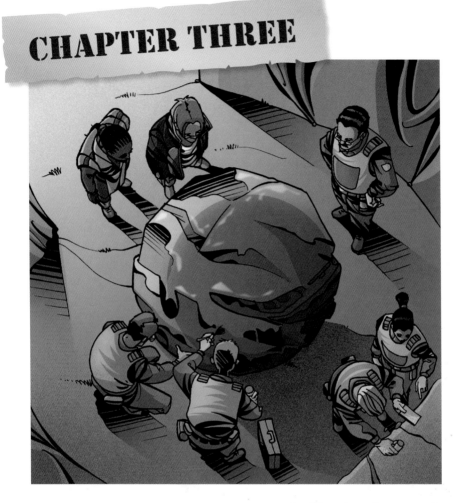

They drove to the scene of the crash. The fog from the night before had gone and it was a lovely sunny day. Parker and Turnbull went into the tent where the forensic team were working on the car wreck. In the daylight it looked like a giant ball of melted chocolate.

"There's something that I really need you to see," said the Head of the Crash Team.

He took them outside the tent and showed them some burn marks on the grass. They led directly into the lake.

"What do you think made these marks?" asked Parker.

"I don't know. But whatever it was, it gave off a great heat. Maybe it was responsible for melting the car," said the Head of the Crash Team.

"I think we should take a look around," Agent Turnbull said. "Whatever made this burn mark might still be here."

As the agents walked towards the lake, several helicopters appeared above them. Within two minutes, there were soldiers all over the road. Parker bent down to look into the lake. He thought he could see a strange dark shape under the water.

He was about to take a photograph with his mobile phone, when a hand touched his shoulder. A soldier took him by the arm. He turned around to see Turnbull being led away.

They were taken to the office of General Brown. He looked serious, but when he saw the two agents' identity cards, he suddenly became very friendly.

"It's great to have MI5 on the case," he said.

"Do you want us to bring you up-to-date?" Parker asked. "We've got a possible case of alien abduction here. We're obviously dealing with a very developed life force. The way that car was melted points to advanced technology – probably beyond the nuclear power we have in the 21st century. Shall I go on?"

Just then, the general's
mobile phone rang.
He took the call.
He listened but he did
not say anything. When
he had finished the call,
he spoke to the two
agents again.

"Excellent work, Agents
Turnbull and Parker.
You're welcome to go
back to London now,"
General Brown said.

"Our orders are to
investigate the car crash.
We are here on MI5
business. You have no
authority to tell us to
go!" Turnbull shouted.

"I have the authority of
your boss, Commander Watson," replied
the general. "He is handing the operation over to
the army. Your help is no longer needed."

The soldiers watched while Parker and Turnbull drove away. But they didn't go far. Once they were out of sight they stopped the car.

"I know why they don't want us to work on this case any longer. We're getting too close to the truth," said Parker. "I told you we couldn't trust Commander Watson."

"Parker," said Turnbull, "it's our duty to find out the truth, no matter what. I'm hiring us some equipment. We need to take a proper look in that lake tonight."

CHAPTER FOUR

They returned to the lake after dark. Turnbull had hired diving gear and wet suits.

"We're taking a big risk," Parker said. "Who knows what might happen if they catch us?"

"You said it would be dangerous finding out the truth," Turnbull replied. "We have no choice but to disobey orders."

As they got near the lake, they heard the sound of
noisy engines. The army had put lifting equipment
near the shore and a big searchlight on the lake.

The two agents slipped soundlessly into the water.

"It's so cold," moaned Agent Parker. "I'm going to have a heart attack."

"Don't be silly, Parker, get a grip," Turnbull commanded, trying not to laugh at him.

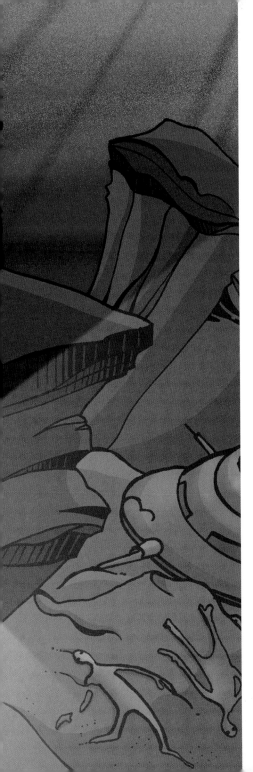

They swam silently along the shoreline and then dived 30 metres away from the army searchlight. Underneath the water it was very clear and their torches worked well.

They stopped next to the wreck of a strange-looking ship. Then Turnbull pulled at Parker's arm and pointed. At the bottom of the lake were the bodies of three strange creatures — three creatures that did not look human.

The agents were about to get closer when they saw four frogmen swimming above them. Turnbull and Parker turned off their torches and waited at the bottom of the lake.

When they got back to the surface, they watched the army divers bring up the bodies of the aliens. Then, the lifting gear brought up the wreck of the spaceship. The soldiers worked silently. They loaded all the evidence into lorries and got ready to drive away.

"Well, that was an interesting night's work," said Turnbull. "But we can't stop now."

"Hang on. What have we learnt?" Parker asked as they climbed out of the lake.

"It's clear that an alien spaceship crashed into the lake. We don't know why that happened but someone in a very high place is trying to cover it up. They don't want anyone to know that an alien life force has been to earth," Laura Turnbull said.

"And Mrs Chivers was almost certainly abducted by aliens before their spaceship crashed into the lake," Parker added.

"We need to follow that lorry," Turnbull said.

"We must find out who or what was in that spaceship. Somehow Mrs Chivers made it out alive. *They* weren't so lucky," Parker replied.

CHAPTER FIVE

Parker and Turnbull followed the lorry down narrow country lanes until they reached an old air force base.

"This is Lampton. I've heard about this place," said Parker. "The army use it as a top-secret base."

The two agents crept up to the fence. Parker used wire cutters to make a hole, just big enough for them to climb through. They headed for the old aircraft hangar. There were no guards and it was easy for them to climb in through a window.

"This is hardly high security," said Turnbull, shining her torch around the hangar.

"It *is* in the middle of nowhere," Parker replied.

He shone his torch onto a dark shape in the corner.

"But if what I can see is what I think it is, they'll be moving this stuff before dawn under armed guard!"

"What is it?" asked Turnbull. "It looks all crusty."

"Turnbull, we're looking at some kind of alien spaceship," he said.

Parker bent down and opened up a body bag.

"Here's the green monster that Mrs Chivers described!" he cried. "Laura, this is one of the most exciting moments of our professional lives!"

Turnbull examined the side of the spaceship.

"Parker, this spaceship was shot down! Look at the holes in its side," she said. "It was attacked by human aircraft. Now I'm feeling nervous."

Parker shivered. "You're right, let's go," he said.
"I'm beginning to understand what might be going
on here."

CHAPTER SIX

When the agents got back to their hotel they both sat in silence.

"What does all this mean?" Turnbull asked.

"I think it means two things," Parker said. "Firstly, the government knows that aliens often visit Earth. There's no way they want ordinary people to know this. Secondly, they're prepared to shoot down alien spaceships and cover up any signs that they have ever visited us."

"And while they're hiding the evidence they're also taking a good look at the alien technology. I bet they're trying to copy it for use on Earth," said Turnbull.

"Most definitely," he replied.

"There's one thing that's bothering me," she said. "What happens to the humans who've been abducted by aliens?"

"They're dangerous people to have around because they know too much. But what they know might also be useful to the Secret Service," Parker explained.

"So what will happen to Mrs Chivers?" Turnbull asked.

"She might get killed in a road accident. Maybe they'll say she's mad and lock her away," he said. "Poor woman, she has no idea what she's involved in now."

"What about me, Parker?" Turnbull whispered. "MI5 know that I have special powers. Look how they used me on the case of the missing scientist, David Minos. I went back in time to save him."

Parker was silent. He remembered the Mind Games Case very well. He shivered as he remembered the deadly creature they had defeated that was half-bull, half-man. It was a long time before he spoke.

"Your life could be in danger too, Laura," he said.

"Parker, you told me the Secret Service put a metal implant in my head. Why did they do that?" she asked. "What do they want from me?"

"I wish I knew the answer," he said. "But they seem to think that you can see into the future as well as the past. You must realise that's why the Secret Service is so interested in you."

Agent Turnbull was silent. There were tears in her eyes. "Parker, I can't live like this," she said. "I must get out of the Secret Service before it's too late."

Parker gave her a hug. He knew he had to be strong for both of them.

"Laura, it is too late already. They won't let you leave. Their interest in you has only just begun."

GLOSSARY OF TERMS

alien abduction
captured by creatures
from outer space

authority permission

evidence proof

Forensic team
investigators looking for
evidence which could be
used in court

frogmen divers

gear equipment

hand over
to give control to

headed for go to

MI5 government
department responsible
for national security

nuclear power
power released by
splitting the atom

orders instructions

Secret Service
Government Intelligence
Department

to cover up
to hide the truth

**very developed
life force**
advanced civilisation

QUIZ

1   Where did the car crash take place?

2   What was the name of the driver?

3   What happened to the spaceship?

4   What did Turnbull hire?

5   Where did the army take the spaceship?

6   What was the most important moment of the agents' professional lives?

7   Why did the government shoot down the alien spaceship?

8   What do the agents think will happen to Mrs Chivers?

9   What did MI5 do to Agent Turnbull's head?

10 What is special about Agent Turnbull?

ABOUT THE AUTHOR

Paul Blum has taught for over 20 years in
London inner-city schools.

I wrote The Extraordinary Files for my pupils so
they've been tested by some fierce critics (you!).
That's why I know you'll enjoy reading them.

I've made the stories edgy in terms of character and
content and I've written them using the kind of fast-
paced dialogue you'll recognise from television soaps.
I hope you'll find The Extraordinary Files an interesting
and easy-to-read collection of stories.

ANSWERS TO QUIZ

1 The Lake District

2 Mrs Chivers

3 It crashed into the lake

4 Diving equipment and wet suits

5 Lampton Air Base

6 When they saw the body of an alien

7a) to stop ordinary people knowing that aliens had come to earth

b) to examine and copy the aliens' advanced technology

8 MI5 will kill her or lock her away

9 They put a metal implant in it

10 She has special powers. She can see into the future as well as the past